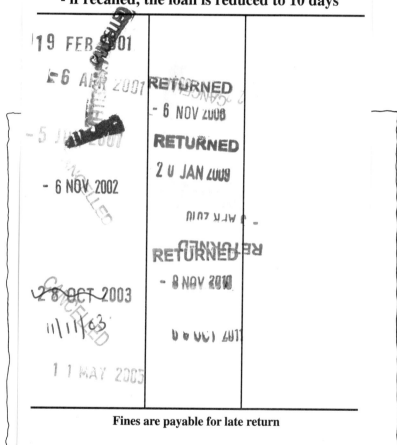

For Yolanda
L.R.

For Rosie
P.L.

First published 1994 by Walker Books Ltd
87 Vauxhall Walk, London SE11 5HJ

This edition published 1996

4 6 8 10 9 7 5 3

Text © 1994 Leon Rosselson
Illustrations © 1994 Priscilla Lamont

The right of Leon Rosselson to be
identified as author of this work has been
asserted by him in accordance with the
Copyright, Designs and Patents Act 1988.

This book has been typeset in New Century Schoolbook.

Printed in Hong Kong/China

British Library Cataloguing in Publication Data
A catalogue record for this book is
available from the British Library.

ISBN 0-7445-4377-0

WHERE'S MY
MUM?

Leon Rosselson
—— illustrated by ——
Priscilla Lamont

WALKER BOOKS
AND SUBSIDIARIES
LONDON • BOSTON • SYDNEY

Where's my mum?

She's not in the drawer,   or under the bed,

or behind the door.

She's not in the bath,

unless she's got

Turned into a spider.

I hope she's not!

I'll look in the mirror;
who can that be
With the scowly face?
It must be me!

She's not in the fridge
with the strawberry jelly,
The chicken, the milk and
the something smelly.

She's not in
the cupboard.
What's that
noise?

No, she's not in the box
with all my toys.

She's not in the piano

or under the chair,

Or behind the curtains

or anywhere.

I'll try the garden.

Where can she be?

She's not in the sky
or the apple tree.

Look at those ants
racing to and fro!
Have you seen my mum?
I think that means no.

I can't see a mum in the garden shed,

And she isn't a flower in the flowerbed!

Perhaps she's in *her* bed.

I'll go and explore.

Back into the house...

Push open her door.

There's a lumpy shape –

I'll take a peep…

There's my mum,

and she's fast asleep!

Mum! Mum!

You should be awake.

Tell me a story!

Bake me a cake!

Mum! I can hop!

I can jump

on the bed!

I can curl in a ball,

I can stand on my head.

Paint me a picture.

Play games
with me.

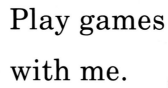

Mum! I'm hungry.
I want my tea.

Can I drink my milk in
my dinosaur mug?

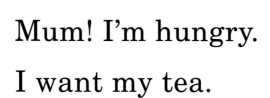

Get up, Mum...

And I'll give you a hug!

MORE WALKER PAPERBACKS
For You to Enjoy

FIRST THINGS FIRST
by Charlotte Voake

Shortlisted for the Smarties Book Prize, this baby's companion
has everything from ABC and 123 to nursery rhymes, fruits and insects.
"Every page is a surprise... This really is the book to catch
your child's attention." *Young Mother*

0-7445-4709-1 £4.99

THREE PICTURE STORIES
by Helen Oxenbury

Each book contains three classic stories of pre-school life,
first published individually as First Picture Books.

"Everyday stories of family life, any one of these humorous depictions
of the trials of an under-five will be readily identified
by children and adults ... buy them all if you can." *Books For Your Children*

0-7445-3722-3   *One Day with Mum*
0-7445-3723-1   *A Bit of Dancing*
0-7445-3724-X   *A Really Great Time*

£3.99 each

OH, LITTLE JACK
by Inga Moore

In this first story about little Jack Rabbit and his family, the young bunny
seems to be too small for everything, until his grandfather saves the day!

"A classic... A real pleasure to read-aloud." *Parents*

0-7445-3126-8   £4.50